Welcome to the Pit!

The underground headquarters of the G.I. Joes is your new home. That's because you are about to become the newest member of the G.I. Joe Team.

Your code name: Spider.

Your major talent: To think fast and make wise decisions under pressure.

Your assignment: Strategy Specialist.

A special G.I. Joe squad is about to go into action. The mission will not be an easy one. As Strategy Specialist, it will be up to you to make sure it is a *successful* one!

Read the directions at the bottom of each page. Then make your decision about what to do next.

If you make the right decisions, the Joe Team will score a triumph over the evil forces of COBRA, and you will be recognized as a hero. If you make the wrong choices, you'll wish you'd never joined the team!!

Good luck, soldier. Begin your mission on page 1.

Another G.I. JOE™ book in
the FIND YOUR FATE™ series
Published by Ballantine Books:

OPERATION: STAR RAIDER

G.I. JOE

OPERATION: DRAGON FIRE

BY WILLIAM SNO

BALLANTINE BOOKS • NEW YORK

RLI: $\dfrac{\text{VL 5 + up}}{\text{IL 6 + up}}$

Copyright © 1985 by Hasbro Inc.
G.I. JOE$_{TM}$: A trademark of Hasbro Inc.
FIND YOUR FATE$_{TM}$: A trademark of Random House, Inc.

Library of Congress Catalog Card Number: 85-90749

ISBN 0-345-32666-0

Cover illustration by Carl Cassler

Illustrated by David Henderson

Editorial Services by Parachute Press, Inc.

Designed by Gene Siegel

Manufactured in the United States of America

First Edition: October 1985

FIND YOUR FATE™®

#2

G.I. JOE

OPERATION: DRAGON FIRE

You are in the monitoring room of the Pit, the underground command center of the G.I. Joe Team. On the computer screen in front of you is a satellite display of the United States. Suddenly the warning panel lights up. The geo-kinetic sensor is flashing *red alert!* Quickly you hit a few keys and zero in on the hot spot. According to the central computer, a large part of South Dakota has just been blown up!

Immediately you alert Hawk, your commanding officer and leader of the team. You give him a quick run-down on the situation.

"Collect all available data," he orders, "and meet me in the briefing room in five minutes."

Back at your station, you start punching away at the computer keyboard. It's plain to everyone in the monitoring room that this was not a simulation or a test. It was the real thing.

Behind you, the high-speed printer spits out readings from the blast site. As the machine clatters away, you prepare yourself for action. The training for the Joe team was intense, so even though somebody has just turned up the flame in the Dakotas, you know that you can stand the heat. You're ready for anything.

When the printout is finished, you fold it under your arm and hop the elevator down to level four.

Turn to page 2.

When you reach the briefing room, you find a G.I. Joe Team already assembled. Hawk introduces each member and details his or her military specialty. To his right is Duke, an airborne infantryman and acting first sergeant. Next is Lady Jaye, covert operations expert with a specialty in intelligence. Rock 'n' Roll is a rock-steady infantryman. Bazooka is a missile specialist, and Barbecue is a firefighter. Leaning against the back wall are Thunder, an artillery specialist, and Roadblock, the heavy machine gunner. You are introduced as Spider, an electronics expert and a skilled martial artist who has trained with Snake-Eyes, the hand-to-hand combat instructor of the Joe Team.

"This," says Hawk abruptly, "is the situation." He activates a satellite film on a wall-sized monitor. The Black Hills of South Dakota come into view. You all watch as the hills are ripped apart and a deep gash is opened in the earth.

"As you can see," Hawk continues, "our country has absorbed an attack by some explosive power, but the source is unknown. We already have advanced intelligence reports, but they offer no explanation for the maximum-duty access surface at the center of the blast site."

You turn to the guy next to you and ask, "What is he talking about?"

Go on to page 3.

"That means that there's a road leading into the blast site," Rock 'n' Roll whispers. "And no one knows how it got there."

"This is the work of the international terrorist group, COBRA," Hawk continues. "Our mission is simple. We investigate the area around the blast site. We uncover the COBRA plot. Then we take the necessary steps to foil the plot. Are there any questions?"

The room is silent.

"All right, check over your gear. We lift off at 0600 hours."

As the team members start to file out of the room, Hawk calls out, "Spider has the latest technical printouts. I want everyone to pick up a copy and study the data."

Roadblock groans. "Hey, Thunder, pick up a copy for me, all right? I've got to go clean my weapon." Reading technical reports is not very popular with some of the team.

Turn to page 10.

3

"I believe your story," you tell Destro, "but a few questions come to mind. First, why blow up a deserted section of South Dakota?"

"That was a small test of explosive power, done under the orders of COBRA Commander," Destro answers.

"That was a *small* test?" Roadblock looks worried.

"What about the second blast?" you ask. "The one that sealed over the entrance?"

"I set off that blast," Destro explains. "I didn't want you to escape once you arrived. I sort of made you my guests here." He pauses. "Actually, I need your help," he continues. "As you know, I am an ordinary weapons dealer. Dragon Fire will put me out of business. Even a simpleminded G.I. Joe will recognize that I couldn't make a profit selling water. So it is imperative that the Dragon Fire system be destroyed.

"At my disposal I have a small band of renegade COBRA fighters. Each is highly motivated, but not one of them is trustworthy. If I am to clash with COBRA Commander, a larger force will be necessary. This is why we must work together. Will you join me in fighting Dragon Fire? I'll supply the COBRA fighters and my expertise, and you'll be able to uncover Operation Dragon Fire."

....

If you agree to help Destro, turn to page 74.
If you refuse Destro, turn to page 40.

4

You decide to join the lead patrol.

You jump out of the jeep after Lady Jaye, the covert operations expert, Roadblock, the machine gunner, and Barbecue, the firefighter. Carefully the four of you pick your way through the rocks to where the earth splits open. There, under an overhanging rock ledge, is the beginning of the prepared gravel road.

Crouching at the entrance, Lady Jaye looks around. "I don't get it," she says. "This area was blasted sky high, but the road is still in good shape."

"I don't care about its condition," says Roadblock. "Why is it here in the first place? I tell you, it looks like a setup and smells like a trap."

"That's why Hawk sent us ahead," you say. "But we're not going to learn anything here."

"Right." Roadblock nods. "You take the lead. You're the best one here with the ground scope. Lady Jaye and Barbecue will back you up, and I'll be watching our tails."

"All right, let's go!" You creep down the rock ledge. "If I see something hairy," you tell the others, "I'm going to radio you on com-channel 47K."

Then you head for the dark cavern.

Turn to page 20.

You remain in the jeep. As the lead patrol begins picking its way down the rocky slope, Hawk shouts, "Start 'em up!" and the main column churns through the dust to the blast site.

The route turns out to be more of a goat path than anything else. With the jeep in low gear and your fingers tight around the roll bar, Hawk noses the jeep toward the edge and down, skidding and sliding the whole way. Somehow, everyone makes it to the bottom.

Hawk signals you to give a radio check to the other vehicles.

You speak into the radio mike. "All units, this is the lead motor. We're going in. Switch radio telecoder to Zebra Blue schedule four. Over."

As the other units check in, you descend into the earth.

Turn to page 24.

Duke leads you along the river to a secluded inlet. Hidden from view, you crouch around in a circle. "After that big explosion, we got separated from the rest of the team," Duke says. "We ended up by this river. This waterway is a busy place. COBRA is using it to move a lot of heavy equipment. Barges and high-speed patrol boats pass by every fifteen minutes."

Rock 'n' Roll points upstream and adds, "We were hidden on a point of land where the barges come in close to shore. We overheard the COBRA workers complaining about the twenty-four-hour work details, and how they couldn't wait for Dragon Fire to be finished so they could get some R and R."

"Dragon Fire must be what we're after," says Duke. "We know it's somewhere downstream. If we're going to stop it, that's where we'll go."

Roadblock stands up and shakes his legs to straighten out the kinks. He looks at the slimy riverbank and says, "I hope you weren't planning to walk there. It would be faster and more pleasant to sneak onto one of the barges or capture a patrol boat. What do you say, Spider?"

Duke is the acting first sergeant and is in command of your group, but you know he is willing to listen to suggestions.

....

If you want to sneak onto a barge, turn to page 80.

If you'd rather try a patrol boat, turn to page 16.

7

Roadblock finds the adjusting lever and tilts his seat back a notch or two. Then he adjusts his rearview mirrors.

"That's better," he announces proudly. "This COBRA coach is no T-Bird, but I think it will do all right." He reaches under his vest, pulls out a tape, and slips it into his portable player. A driving rhythm fills the APC.

"What are you doing?" you ask. "Are you crazy? Every COBRA within a hundred miles will hear that." You turn to Barbecue. He's tapping his foot and watching the sights. He's seen this all before.

"Spider, my friend," Roadblock says to you, "when you've been on as many missions as I have, you learn to eat when you can, sleep when you can, and listen to the tunes anytime you can hear them over the artillery."

You shake your head in disbelief. It's going to be a lot of fun going into battle with this crew. You keep watch on the surrounding hills as Roadblock fine-tunes the stereo.

Suddenly you hear a piercing whistle over your head. *SKREEE! BLAM!*

"Incoming rockets!" shouts Lady Jaye. Roadblock twists the wheel hard to the right.

....

Turn to page 60.

8

You switch on the radio. "Attention. This is Spider in the lead jeep. Hawk is injured. Armored COBRAS coming our way. Turn over all vehicles. Let's make it look like that blast did us in."

As the others follow your orders, you check on Hawk. He's come to and doesn't seem seriously hurt. The COBRAS are only a hundred yards away now. You creep back to the wrecked jeep. Safely hidden underneath, you wait.

Slowly the armored column passes by. A COBRA trooper walks around the jeep, but he doesn't check it carefully. Thunder has set a wrecked COBRA APC (armored personnel carrier) on fire. It was a smart move and attracts a lot of COBRA attention. Two more jeeps pass by your position. Then the APC that's bringing up the rear pulls up by your jeep. The COBRA in the left front seat looks like the column leader. You roll out from under the jeep and dive into the APC, nailing the driver with a powerful side kick and sending him flying over the windshield. A split second later your machine pistol is behind the column leader's ear. You bend over him and whisper, "Cool out, COBRA. This column has just been captured."

Turn to page 32.

9

At 0600 sharp, the G.I. Joe Team lifts off. A few hours later the C-130 transport plane touches down at an abandoned airstrip in the hills of South Dakota. You climb into the lead jeep with Hawk, Barbecue, and Lady Jaye and rumble down a barren dirt road to the edge of the blast site. The other jeeps follow.

"You're not going to sell a lot of postcards of this place!" says Hawk.

You look out over four square miles of jagged rock. In the center, a deep split is slashed through the earth's crust. Just visible is a smooth gravel road.

"It looks like an earthquake," says Lady Jaye. "But the rock structure is all wrong. It couldn't have happened naturally."

"COBRA isn't natural," says Hawk. He scans the terrain with his binoculars. "I see a route down the western edge where we can gain access to that road, but I want a lead patrol to check things out for the main column. Any volunteers?"

Roadblock, Barbecue, and Lady Jaye step forward.

. . . .

If you want to volunteer to join the lead patrol, turn to page 5.

If you decide to stay with the main column, turn to page 6.

10

"Floor it, Roadblock!" you shout.

"This *is* floored!" he yells back.

"Oh no," you mutter. It figures that you would swipe a carrier in need of a tune-up. No wonder it was the last one in the COBRA column. "I guess I'll have to try to slow them down some," you say. "Barbecue, give me a hand racking up the machine gun." The two of you climb to the back.

You squeeze off an entire case of ammo. It barely puts a dent in the lead H.I.S.S. tank. You clip in the next belt and line up your target anyway. But before you can pull the trigger—*WHOOMPF!* The lead tank bursts into flames. Then the second tank slams into the wreckage of the first, pushing it over the edge and down into the ravine.

"Good shootin'!" says Roadblock. "How did you do it?"

"I didn't do anything," you say. "I was reloading."

"That tank was hit by an incendiary rocket that was fired from up there." Barbecue points to a position on a cliff about two miles away.

Turn to page 27.

Very carefully you move deeper into the underground COBRA nest. With each step, your boots crunch on the gravel road. You would feel a lot better if you had some backup, but if you're on your own, well, that's just the way it is. You'll do what you can to complete the mission.

Every second, you're watching the hills, watching the road, watching the ravine, looking for anything that might give away a hostile position.

You've had years of training in the martial arts and you're a smart nighttime fighter—but you're no match for the band of COBRA troopers that jump you as you edge around a rocky outcropping.

"Gimme a break," you say to the troopers. But they grin evilly. As they draw their weapons, you know that this first mission is your last.

THE END

You ram right through the doors and find yourselves navigating down a COBRA corridor at just a notch under top speed. You clip off a string of lights that hangs from the ceiling, cut around a corner, and almost flatten a squad of troopers. You expect them to fire at you, but they don't.

"I don't know," says Thunder. "Maybe they race tanks through this place *every* afternoon."

"Get serious, Thunder. We've got to find the central control room. Do you have any ideas?"

Thunder switches the forward observation screen to wide angle and says, "Sure, like anybody else we'll either follow the signs or ask for directions. For instance—will you slow down! I'm having trouble reading these—that one says 'High-Security Area,' and just up ahead there's a sign pointing to 'Lower Level III.' It's up to you."

If you want to check out the High-Security Area, turn to page 56.

If you'd rather investigate Lower Level III, turn to page 48.

14

You grip the roll bar. You're not going to let go, no matter how rough it gets. As the APC plows down the ravine, Roadblock does his best to keep it upright.

"A little to your right," says Barbecue.

Roadblock ignores his helpful advice. A shower of sparks shoot up into the air as the APC's right side scrapes along a large rock. "Watch it on the left!" Lady Jaye shouts.

"I don't think he's listening," you say to Lady Jaye.

"I guess he's got his hands full," she answers.

Roadblock is staring straight ahead, twisting the wheel like a wild man. After a few more seconds the ground flattens out and the APC finally coasts to a stop at the edge of a river. Except for a few rocks sliding down the ravine, everything is quiet.

The four of you pause and listen carefully. There's not a sound. You lost them!

Suddenly a quiet voice from behind you says, "Coming down a hill like that, you people are a dangerous bunch." You whirl around. Where did that come from?

Turn to page 34.

15

"I know how to get us a patrol boat," you say. Duke nods. He'll go along with your idea. You lead the team back to the COBRA APC.

"First we need somebody who can put on a good act. You, Roadblock. I want you to lie down with your legs sticking out from under the APC and groan."

Roadblock's brow wrinkles, but there's a gleam in his eye.

Turning to Duke, Barbecue, and Rock 'n' Roll, you say, "Your position is over there in the water. Stay low behind the rocks. Lady Jaye and I will be up there on the bank. When the next patrol boat comes by, it'll dock so COBRA can check out the APC. They'll see Roadblock and think he's a wounded COBRA. When they come ashore, they'll be right in the middle of our trap."

Roadblock shakes his head and says, "You've got me lying in the dirt and these two guys sitting over there in the water. Without a doubt, Spider, this isn't one of your better plans."

"Trust me," you say.

Turn to page 64.

16

"But the name Dragon Fire isn't enough," says Duke.

"Well, whatever it is," says Bazooka, "we know it's important enough for an entire COBRA unit to take a knockout shot. They knew something they didn't want leaked out."

"Right," says Duke, "and we'll get on it as soon as we get this unit back into action. Thunder, Bazooka, Rock 'n' Roll, check over our vehicles. If they run, get them ready to move out. If we're a little shy on transportation, just borrow something from our local COBRA motor pool.

"Spider, see what you can find in the column leader's APC. I'm going to see how Hawk and the others are doing."

You trot back to the last APC and switch on the topographic locator that's mounted in the center console. Your present position is shown on the screen. Around it is a map of the surrounding area. One corner of the screen is blank. It could be an electronic defect. You zoom in on it. Not a chance. That part of the data base has been erased—and probably for a very good reason.

Turn to page 58.

17

"Let's get out of here before those COBRAS change their minds and start firing on us," you say.

Roadblock starts up the APC. You've only gone a few feet when half a dozen rockets explode in a circle around you. Roadblock hits the brakes. "They could have nailed us easily!" he says. "But they didn't. That sounds like an invitation we can't ignore."

"If that's the case," says Lady Jaye, slinging her weapon over her shoulder, "let's pay them a little visit."

Turn to page 33.

Using the instruments in the COBRA APC, you lead the Joe Team to a spot high on a mountainous ridge. You check the screen one more time. "This is the place," you announce.

"Well, they must have it well camouflaged," says Duke. "I don't see anything but rock."

He steps out of the APC and walks to the edge of the ridge. Something catches his eye. He checks it out with his binoculars and then motions for you to have a look.

Below you, almost buried in the rock, is a long, low concrete building. Three sides are protected by a wall. Its rear is up against a cliff.

Duke calls the others over. "This has all the signs of being COBRA Command Center," he says. "Their Dragon Fire operation, whatever it is, has got to be inside. I want two separate teams to go in. The first will be a two-man unit that will rappel down the cliff and enter the compound from the back. The second unit will move down the ridge and attack from the side."

If you decide to join the two-man unit, turn to page 69.

If you decide to join the large force, turn to page 28.

19

You crawl forty feet down into the cavern and lower yourself off the rock ledge and onto the road. You switch on your infrared goggles for a better view. With them, you can see that this cavern opens up into a huge underground world. To the right, the terrain rises in a series of cliffs. To the left, it falls away from the road.

You unstrap the ground scope from your battle pack. When properly used, its reading will help you to detect troop movements and mechanized activity. Just as you switch it on, the ground begins to shake. A terrifying roar fills the cavern. Rocks and debris fly through the air. The dust is so thick that your infrared goggles are useless. But the ground scope picks up no sign of life.

You switch your radio to com-channel 47K and try to raise Roadblock or Barbecue or Lady Jaye. Nothing but static. Next you try Hawk and the main column. Silence.

Should you search for the rest of the lead patrol? Or try to rejoin the main column? Or continue deeper into COBRA territory . . . alone?

. . . .

If you decide to search for Roadblock, Lady Jaye, and Barbecue, turn to page 36.

If you decide to rejoin the main column, turn to page 86.

If you choose to go into COBRA territory alone, turn to page 13.

20

Roadblock and Lady Jaye slide over the edge of the road and down into the ravine. You and Barbecue dive after them, skidding to a stop alongside Roadblock.

"Keep down," cautions Lady Jaye. "We don't have much cover here. If they look over the edge, they'll spot us."

Everyone squirms a little flatter against the ground. In the pit of your stomach you can feel the vibration of the approaching armor.

Roadblock lifts his head. "Those are heavy-duty H.I.S.S. tanks rolling by. It'll be hard to outshoot them, but it'd sure be nice to have some wheels."

"We may have to trick them," Lady Jaye says. "I'm going to get closer. When the last vehicle comes into view, you'll hear me raising a fuss. That's the signal for you three to come up top and do something appropriate."

"Well, at least she's got all the details worked out," Barbecue says.

Turn to page 73.

Destro turns and strides off toward the COBRA camp, his cape swirling behind him. Barbecue steps closer to you and whispers, "I don't like this. Destro is so unscrupulous, even COBRA doesn't trust him."

Roadblock nods. "He'll sell anything to anyone."

"All right. We'll keep our eyes open," you say. "But we've got to crack this COBRA plot, and we're not going to unless we go along with him." You pick up your battle pack and follow Destro.

He leads you through the outer edge of the camp, past four COBRA guards, through an inner checkpoint that's protected by mobile armored panels, then into a reinforced bunker. You make a mental note of every detail. Something is going to happen, and you want to be ready.

Destro pauses by a wrinkled map that's taped to the wall, then he turns and says, "This is the situation...Where are the others? Why aren't they here?"

"Relax, Destro," says Barbecue as he enters the bunker. "We haven't missed anything...because you haven't said anything interesting yet."

"Silence!" Destro orders. "A situation has developed that threatens your existence as well as mine. What I am about to reveal is critical to our survival."

Turn to page 35.

Just a hundred yards in from the entrance the sunlight has grown so dim that you must switch on your infrared night-vision scope. As you drive deeper into the earth, a rugged, mountainous landscape looms out of the darkness.

"There's an entire world down here," says Hawk in amazement. "Still, I wish this road weren't here. It makes me feel like someone is waiting for us."

You check the surface range scope (SRS) to see if you can get a reading on any hostile activity. Suddenly the ground begins to shake and roll. A COBRA column must be approaching! A deafening roar tears through the darkness. *BLAM!* Tons of rock crash down around you. One boulder catches the rear quarter panel of your jeep and flips it into the air. You go flying out, landing hard on the ground.

When your head clears, you survey the situation. Hawk is unconscious. The jeep has been destroyed. A few of the other vehicles are damaged, and some of your teammates may be hurt. You check your SRS. The readings indicate that an armored column is approaching.

Should you try to revive Hawk? Or should you radio the backup Joe Team?

....

If you try to revive Hawk, turn to page 47.
If you radio the backup, turn to page 9.

Like a hawk coming out of the sky, you leap over the side and attack. As you strike the pressure point between the third and fourth vertebrae, your prey crumples to the floor. You sling COBRA Commander over your shoulder and start back to the tank. By staying between the rows of equipment, you make it unnoticed.

Thunder is waiting for you. "It couldn't have been done any neater," he says. Together you drop COBRA Commander inside the tank. "That takes care of the dragon. Now all we have to do is get out of this place," says Thunder.

"Just a second," you say. "I have one more little errand. I'll be right back."

You make your way unseen to the main computer.

You press one button.

The screen goes blank.

You return to Thunder.

"What was that all about?" he asks.

"I just erased all information pertaining to Operation Dragon Fire. Our mission is over. We uncovered the COBRA plot and foiled it as well."

Thunder grins at you. "Let's get out of here!" he says.

THE END

"Roadblock!" you shout. "Cut down into the ravine. It's getting too hot up here!"

Roadblock swerves around a crater and says, "That ravine can't be any worse than this road. Hang on!" He launches the APC over the edge. The tracks spin as you fly through the air.

"Oh no, here it comes!" The APC slams into the ground. It skids hard to the right. Roadblock fights for control. A huge boulder rams up under the right track. Lady Jaye is almost thrown out of her seat.

"I don't think I can hold it together much longer!" Roadblock shouts.

Just to the left of your seat is the emergency braking system switch. You could reach down and activate it. Maybe it would help. Or maybe you should just hang on and hope.

If you decide to hit the brake, turn to page 63.

If you decide to hang on and hope, turn to page 15.

"Spider, see if you can get some readouts on that position," says Roadblock.

You pull the ground scope out of your pack and dial it in to the cliff top. Your eyes can't pick out any movement, but the electronic circuitry sees plenty. When the data is fully analyzed, you let out a low whistle. "You're not going to believe this," you say, "but all indications point to one thing: a mobile COBRA observation camp with at least two missile launchers that each have ground-oriented heat-sensing capability."

Roadblock's brow wrinkles with confusion. "Get serious," he says. "I was hoping it was Hawk and the others."

"Apparently not," says Lady Jaye. "For some reason, COBRA forces are firing on COBRA forces. If we can find out why they're firing on their own people, it might explain what they're up to."

"I still don't like the idea of climbing into a COBRA camp," says Roadblock, "even if they did shoot a couple of tanks off our tail. What do you think, Spider? Should we be heroes and check it out or be smart and slip on by?

. . . .

If you decide to check it out, turn to page 33.
If you'd rather avoid trouble, turn to page 18.

27

You join the large team and move down the ridge. The terrain is rough enough to provide good cover, but when you get to the bottom it smooths out. Between you and Command Center is nothing but open ground.

"I don't think they know we're here," says Duke. "We may be able to make it to the wall without a shot being fired. Everyone ready?" Your teammates give the sign. "All right, let's go!"

You tear across the open ground, ready for the battle to start. But you've caught COBRA by surprise. With your heart pounding, you reach the wall.

The others catch up. Rock 'n' Roll tosses the grappling hooks into place, and you scale the wall. As you drop to the inside, the compound erupts in noise. *KA-BLAM! BOOM! RAT-A-TAT-A-TAT!* You couldn't hear an order if one were given. You have to rely on your extensive training.

Furiously you fight your way inside the Command Center.

"Up here!" calls Duke. "They're inside this room!"

Everyone races down the corridor to Duke's position. He's got someone trapped in the room. Diving past the doorway, you toss in a grenade. *BA-ROOM!* Just after it blows, you all charge in.

Turn to page 72.

Without any real idea of where you're going, the four of you feel your way deeper into the cavern. Every few minutes you check the scanning equipment, but it doesn't see any better than you can.

"Hey, Spider," Roadblock whispers, "when was the last time you ate?"

"Why do you want to know?" you ask. "Are you planning to cook a gourmet meal for us?"

"I just wondered if what I heard was your stomach rumbling." He turns to the others. "What about your stomachs?"

"They're quiet, Roadblock," they reply.

"Well, then, that rumbling can only be one thing: There's an armored column closing in, and I can guarantee that it's COBRA." Now that he's mentioned it, you can just barely hear the distant sound of half-tracked troop carriers.

"They are still a few minutes away," calculates Lady Jaye. "Just enough time to get ready. If we climb a little way up those cliffs, we'll have a direct shot at them when they come into view."

Roadblock considers the plan and then says, "Or we could wait for them in the ravine, and when they pass by, jump 'em! What do you think, Spider?"

....

If you want to take them from the cliffs, turn to page 55.

If you want to jump them from the ravine, turn to page 22.

29

Duke pulls back on the throttle, the engines howl, and you race in toward the docks. You see COBRA workers unloading crates marked DRAGON FIRE. Some of the barges are being guarded by armed COBRA troopers. It all looks very secret and very sinister.

"They can't be up to any good," you say, eyeing the guards and remembering the blast you saw.

"Yeah," growls Rock 'n' Roll. "I don't know what Dragon Fire is, but we'd better get rid of it."

"Right!" says Duke. He cuts around the barges. Roadblock and Rock 'n' Roll open up with their .50s. They splinter the wooden packing crates and everything inside them. *RAT-A-TAT-A-TAT!*

Wheeling around, Duke heads toward the fuel dump. He closes in at full speed, then at the last second pulls into reverse. The twin props churn in the water. He cuts the wheel hard to the right and the boat spins around. You pop off four depth charges and pull out just as they blow!

"For you, COBRA!" roars Roadblock.

Turn to page 89.

"I will instruct my men to prepare themselves for your orders," he hisses. Slowly he raises his gloved hand to the radio transmitter strapped around his throat. "All COBRA troopers: Complete your mission!" His hand darts to a red button mounted on the side of the transmitter. You try to stop him, but he's too fast. He pushes it, activating an injection. Instantly, he slumps over in his seat, unconscious!

You glance around at the other COBRAS. It's the same thing. How are you going to conduct interrogations when they're all dropping like flies?

It's only a knockout injection. But you have no way of knowing how long they'll stay under. It could be days. You spot a huge COBRA trooper staggering around. You leap out of the APC and run toward him calling, "Duke, Thunder, Bazooka, anybody! Bring the medi-kit. Fast!"

When you reach the COBRA trooper, he's fallen to the ground. A second later—*WHOOSH!* Thunder slides alongside him. He's already got the kit open. Duke pulls up the COBRA's sleeve. "Give him a shot of adrenaline. We've got to keep him awake." As Thunder works on him, Duke leans down and tells the COBRA, "You're in the COBRA debriefing center. Report your mission, report your mission."

With a slurred voice the COBRA trooper responds, "Dragon Fire."

You look at Duke. "That could be it!"

Turn to page 17.

32

The four of you jump out of the APC and begin the difficult trek up through the cliffs. Lady Jaye is in front, climbing almost effortlessly. She leaps from one rock to the next as if she were a cat. Roadblock is behind, dragging the heavy machine gun. Every time he comes to a difficult spot you can hear him mutter something about his heavy load. But you know he would never leave it behind.

After about an hour Lady Jaye signals that she's nearly at the top. You and Barbecue catch up to her. By the time Roadblock has reached her, she's flattened against the ground, looking through her field glasses. "There's a camp over there."

"Let's stay right here," Roadblock says, dropping his gear on the ground. "I've got to catch my breath."

"And well you should!" A deep voice echoes off the rocks.

The four of you turn around. A tall man stands over you. His face is hidden by a silver battle mask.

It's Destro! He's COBRA's biggest weapons supplier—but he's not a loyal COBRA. He'll provide weapons to anyone and fight on any side that suits him.

"Who did you expect? An insignificant COBRA corporal, perhaps?" Destro smirks. "Follow me!"

Turn to page 23.

You, Barbecue, and Lady Jaye dive out of the jeep, hit the ground, roll behind a boulder, and jump to your feet. Your machine pistols are cocked. Roadblock hops off the back of the APC and calls out in an irritated voice, "Don't fool with me now! I've had a trying day."

A voice not too far away says, "Keep your voices down and don't shoot. We're coming out into the open." Two figures rise up from the ground and walk slowly toward you.

"It's Duke and Rock 'n' Roll!" Lady Jaye whispers.

"Where did you guys come from?" you ask.

"I'll explain everything later," says Duke as he reaches you. "But first we've got to get away from that rattle-trap truck. It draws too much attention."

Turn to page 7.

"COBRA forces, under the leadership of COBRA Commander, have been working feverishly on an operation code-named Dragon Fire," Destro begins. "In spite of the close association that I have with those fighters, I was told nothing about this project. I only know of its existence because I have a well-placed spy in COBRA Command Center. I have learned that Dragon Fire is a plot to terrorize the world into submitting to COBRA Commander's rule."

"How does COBRA plan to accomplish that?" asks Barbecue.

"Geothermally," replies Destro smugly.

"Geothermal," you think aloud. "It means heat from the earth."

"Exactly," says Destro. "The heat from the earth's molten core combined with just one other material will create the most massively destructive weapon that you can imagine."

Turn to page 84.

You begin the search for Roadblock, Barbecue, and Lady Jaye. The readings from the ground scope are being fouled up by all the dust that's hanging in the air, so you can't use it to help locate the lead patrol. Luckily, the scope does show the direction you were walking before the blast. If you retrace your steps, maybe you'll find the lead patrol.

You give it a try. Suddenly you hear something in front of you. Was it a rock falling off the cliff? Could it be the rubble shifting and settling?

Ten feet away, two large forms appear out of the dust. It's Roadblock and Barbecue.

"If you were COBRA, you'd be dead meat," Barbecue says.

"If *you* were COBRA, you'd be in more pieces than a jigsaw puzzle," you reply with a grin. "Where's Lady Jaye?"

"Back here." Her voice comes through the dust. "I was following Roadblock and Barbecue to make sure they didn't get lost."

"I never get lost," Roadblock says. "But I wish I knew where the enemy is!"

"Come on," says Lady Jaye. "A little thing like that never stopped us." She strides ahead into the gloom.

....

Turn to page 29.

"I need a moment to think," you say.

"You may have that," Destro answers.

You step to the back of the room and review the situation: There was the destruction of several square miles of South Dakota, the prepared road, the COBRA tanks that were shot off your tail. It could all make sense except for one thing—why would the COBRA troopers fire on their own men?

It doesn't add up, unless it is all just a trick. You didn't actually *see* anyone in those tanks. They could have been robotically controlled. It could have been a simple gag to lure you into Destro's camp. Why? Perhaps so he could brainwash you and then use you as the bait to lure the others into the same trap. The process might have already started. You look over at Roadblock and Barbecue and Lady Jaye. They were out of your sight for a minute or two when you walked to the bunker. Did Destro get to them? Is that why they're going along with this so easily? There's not much time. You have to make a decision: Should you try to escape and save yourself? Or should you jump Destro and save your friends before they fall completely under his control?

If you decide to escape alone, turn to page 44.
If you decide to jump Destro, turn to page 77.

At 1750 hours you, Roadblock, Barbecue, and Lady Jaye are waiting at the outer perimeter of Destro's camp.

Barbecue's feet are propped up on an armored panel. His eyes are closed, but his ears are open. "I hear them coming," he says.

Sure enough, a few moments later a few hundred tons of tracked fire power roll up alongside you.

Hawk hops out of the lead jeep and strides over to you. "What's the lead patrol got to report?" he asks.

As the G.I. Joe Team gathers around, you do your best to summarize the situation. You explain how you hooked up with Destro, and you run through the intelligence on Dragon Fire.

Hawk frowns when you describe Destro's plan to work together against the COBRA forces. "It's like walking around with a hornet in your pocket," he says. "Not very smart, but if you've got a good reason, you do it anyway. Destro has information on Dragon Fire that we need. We're helping him as much as he's helping us. And I want everyone to remember: Destro isn't COBRA, but he *definitely* isn't a Boy Scout."

Barbecue stands up and stretches. "With that in mind," he says, "let's go meet the man."

Go on to page 39.

Destro is waiting as the Joe Team files into his bunker. It's a cramped fit, but everyone squeezes around the central table. All eyes are on the hand-drawn map.

"This is what is known about COBRA Command Center," Destro begins. "It is located here, on the high ground. To the west is a deep gorge. A small river runs through it. There are artillery and rocket positions located on the ridge. As you can see, they are perfectly placed to protect the main entrance, which is here."

Destro pauses to look around the room. Everyone is paying close attention; their lives will depend on this briefing. Destro continues: "This is the main building. It is heavily fortified with a specially hardened concrete. The Dragon Fire control center is located underground in a high-security area. We must enter it in order to stop the COBRA plot. I propose that we neutralize the heavy artillery that protects the area."

Everyone agrees.

Turn to page 66.

You walk up to Destro and stand eyeball to eyeball with him. "Do you expect us to join up with a renegade COBRA outfit run by a fast-talking, double-edged gunrunner? The answer is *no*, end of discussion!" As you turn, Destro's fist flashes out. You see it just in time to catch it and pull him off balance. Then, spinning around, you drive your knee into his stomach. As he doubles over and sinks to the ground, four guards jump you from behind and pin you to the floor.

Gasping for breath, Destro says, "Take them to the communications bunker. Secure them and activate the automatic transmitter. We're breaking camp!"

His orders are quickly carried out. You, Roadblock, Barbecue, and Lady Jaye are taken to the bunker and chained to an abandoned armored panel. Destro's men remove your weapons. A small emergency transmitter is switched on to COBRA frequency 12.

As Destro and his men prepare to move out, you consider your options. You can't escape, and the backup probably won't pick up the COBRA radio signal. But maybe you could reason with Destro, try to convince him that you've changed your mind. It might just work, but are you really prepared to plead for your life?

Give it a try on page 59.

You lift yourself up and stagger to the screen. Incredible—it looks like a computer city! You see row after row of high-speed printers, monitors, and analyzers. Overhead is a network of pipes, transformers, and generators. Even inside the tank, you can hear the hum of all the machinery.

"Look!" Thunder grabs your arm as he scans the screen to the right. "See that man standing by the monitor? It's COBRA Commander. He's the power behind Dragon Fire."

You increase the magnification. Sure enough, even though his back is toward you, COBRA Commander's silhouette is unmistakable. He's wearing his featureless mask and odd, bowl-shaped helmet. You are looking at a fanatical ruler, the most terrifying the world has ever known.

COBRA Commander is completely absorbed by what he sees on the screen. You double the magnification. He's watching the Team Joes battle his men throughout the entire compound.

You look at Thunder and say, "I think we should take the fight right into his back pocket. Keep the engine running...just in case. I've got a job to do!"

You unlace your boots and pull them off. Next you remove all your weapons. They would simply get in the way.

With a final nod to Thunder, you climb out of the tank.

....

Turn to page 65.

You join the line of COBRA workers who are wheeling the crates inside. You follow them deep into Command Center and deliver the stuff to Broadcast Room I. When the workers leave to pick up another load, you and Bazooka hang back. The door closes. You're alone.

"Check this out," says Bazooka. He taps on a thick glass wall that separates you from a huge room full of computers.

"If we could pull the plug on this, their operation would be shut down for sure!" you say. Two guards walk past, and you and Bazooka dive for cover under a rack of equipment.

"It would be easy if we had a few tons of explosives," Bazooka mutters.

Suddenly you get an idea. "We might not need it!" you say.

Turn to page 83.

43

The entrance to the bunker is only four paces away. Without warning, you dive through it to the ground outside. Destro lunges after you, firing several shots, but you roll away and come up running.

You leap over the first checkpoint, then the next, and clear the outer perimeter. A dozen COBRA troopers are firing at you, the bullets screaming off the rocks, but the cliff is just ahead. As the bullets ricochet off the rocks around you, you reach the cliff and disappear over the edge.

Hours later you meet up with the G.I. Joe main column. You explain Operation Dragon Fire to Hawk.

"Men!" Hawk addresses the team. "We have the information we need. We know what the COBRA plot is. Now we must thwart it."

He barks out orders.

"Okay, move out!" he yells. He turns to you. "Good work, G.I. Joe." You grin and join your teammates as they infiltrate COBRA territory, ready to save the world from the clutches of evil.

THE END

The bullets dance into the ground, but somehow you make it to the abandoned tank. You leap onto the top, then drop through the hatch to the inside.

Thunder drops in alongside you and says, "Not gonna last long sitting here like this. That tank in front of us was destroyed by a direct hit, and I don't know if we've got room enough to back up! What do you want to do, Spider?"

If you decide to turn around and try to regroup with the rest of the G.I. Joe Team, turn to page 52.

If you decide to try to climb over the wrecked tank in front of you, turn to page 71.

45

Destro takes you to the communications bunker. "You haven't been successful in contacting your main column because of the heavy ionization factor," he explains. "This equipment, however, will get through. Give it a try."

You sit down at the transmitter and dial up the proper frequency. Working in code, you send the following message:

LEAD PATROL TO MAIN COLUMN.
UNDERSTAND COBRA PLOT. MEET AT THIS LOCATION.

You finish with your identification number.

A few seconds later the response comes back:

GOOD WORK. E.T.A. 1750 HOURS.

"It's all set," you announce. "They'll be here in"—you glance at your watch—"about two hours."

"All right," says Roadblock. "How about some chow? It seems about time."

"Easily arranged," says Destro. He calls outside and one of his men comes running. "Show our new allies to the mess tent," he orders. As you, Roadblock, Barbecue, and Lady Jaye file outside, he adds, "Take your time, but be ready by 1750."

Turn to page 38.

Hawk is lying beside the wrecked jeep. He is no longer unconscious, but his eyes are glazed. You splash some water from your canteen on his face. Then you search for his medi-kit, but you can't find it. It must have been thrown free when the jeep flipped over. Frantically you search the area around you. You crawl along on your hands and knees, pushing aside the debris. You've got to find the kit.

Desperately you pry up a large slab of rock. You've found it! As you reach for the small metal box, a voice behind you says, "G.I. Joe, freeze."

From the corner of your eye you see a COBRA trooper standing over you. His machine gun is ready.

You were so busy looking for the medi-kit that you forgot about the approaching COBRA column. And you didn't alert the others.

Without a shot being fired, the entire G.I. Joe Team are taken prisoners. Your mission is over before it begins. You haven't even uncovered the COBRA plot. Maybe the lead patrol will be more successful.

THE END

Thunder didn't tell you that the sign for Lower Level III was pointing down a flight of stairs. But it doesn't matter. With one side of the tank gouging out the wall and the other bending over the handrail, you thump on down to the lower level. There's a tight turn at the bottom, and you chew your way around it.

A few feet in front of you, the passageway ends in a blank wall. Suddenly an armor-piercing shell explodes to your right.

"A dozen COBRAS coming up from behind!" yells Thunder. He sprays the stairwell with machine-gun fire. *RAT-A-TAT-A-TAT-A-TAT!* "If we get stuck here, we're gone for good!" he yells.

"There's only one way out," you say. Pushing the twenty tons of H.I.S.S. tank up to top speed, you charge down the passageway and ram straight into the wall. The impact is tremendous. It sends you flying out of your seat.

"Did we get through?" you ask, feeling a little dazed.

Thunder checks the forward-viewing screen and says, "We sure did, but you won't believe what I'm seeing."

. . . .
Turn to page 42.

48

You all check over your equipment while keeping a sharp eye on Destro's men. You don't trust them completely, but so far, so good.

You and Thunder are in charge of the communications truck. Quickly you and the others load up and move out. There's nothing delicate about this part of the operation, just steel tracks and high explosives.

As you get closer to COBRA Command Center, Duke radios you and asks you to monitor the COBRA radio frequencies. From your station in the communications truck that's easily done.

The first time you scan the channels, everything is quiet. But the second time you run through, the COBRA chatter is thick and furious! Patching the output from the monitor through the digital analyzer, you get a good idea of what they're saying. You radio Duke and report, "COBRA forces are gearing up. They know we're coming!"

"It doesn't matter," says Thunder, cutting in on your headset. "We're on a roll!"

Turn to page 51.

49

You bump down the road, trying to keep the electronic equipment from shaking itself to death.

"There it is!" says Thunder.

You press your face against the small observation window and can barely make it out. Set just below the top of the mountain ridge is the COBRA Command Center. It's a huge complex. And somewhere underground, according to Destro, in a high-security area, is the Dragon Fire control center.

"It looks like it was carved out of solid rock," says Thunder as he tightens the strap on his helmet. "I guess we'll just have to soften it up."

The plan is for Destro's men to use tanks to make a run for the fortified entrance. The rest of the team will peel off to the side and pound the dust out of the COBRA guns that are mounted on top of the ridge. You and Thunder are to man the electronics truck and patch communications from Destro's men through to the Joe Team.

Like clockwork, Destro's tanks make their move. But the COBRA forces are ready, and they open up with everything that fires. *POW! POW! BLAM!* All you can hear are explosions and gunfire. But the G.I. Joe Team holds its own against the heavy artillery.

Suddenly a message comes in from one of the tanks: TROUBLE UP FRONT...TWO TANKS...TROUBLE...

Turn to page 76.

51

"Hang on, Thunder," you say. "We're turning around." You lock the right track and put the left one in a fast spin. *ZOOM!* The tank whips around to the right, then suddenly climbs up at a crazy angle. Thunder topples to the floor. You're left dangling on the controls.

"You're climbing the tank behind us!" he shouts. "Bring us down!"

You jam the hydraulic controls into reverse, but it's too late. The M-90 balances on one track for just a second and then crashes over onto its side. The unarmored belly of the tank is now facing straight toward the COBRA wall. You and Thunder wind up in a tangle on the floor.

Outside, one of the COBRA troopers guarding the wall smiles, then takes careful aim with his rocket.

"Okay, G.I. Joe!" he yells. "I'm going to do COBRA Commander a favor and finish you off!"

He lets loose the rocket.
KA-BLAMM!

THE END

"Until I get a change in orders, I'm going to stay right here!" you tell Thunder.

He nods. "You can't go wrong following orders."

The two of you bury yourselves in the communications equipment. The messages between Destro and the G.I. Joe Team are flying so fast that you can barely keep up with them. You just finish relaying the COBRA target coordinates to your teammates on the left wing when something comes in about a position being overrun. You can't hear who it is. You're not even sure who sent the message.

Suddenly someone starts banging on the back door of the truck. "What do you want?" you yell. You throw open the door and two COBRA troopers push their submachine guns into your faces.

"I don't want either one of you," the lead officer says, "but since you're my prisoners, I'll have to take you."

Thunder raises his hands over his head and says, "Well, at least we know who got overrun."

You pound your fist into an instrument panel. You got so close! You uncovered the COBRA plot and found the COBRA Command Center. Maybe Destro and the others will be able to complete the mission. But right now you're about to help a couple of no-good troopers make brownie points with COBRA Commander.

THE END

"It's about time this COBRA business was brought to an end," you say. "Let's move out now."

"An excellent decision," says Destro, removing the map from the wall and rolling it up.

Just then one of his men enters and says, "Urgent message from Sector Seven, sir."

Destro's eyes light up as he examines the message. Then he says, "My COBRA spy has just informed me that there is new intelligence on Dragon Fire. A meeting has been set up for 1650 hours."

At 1650 hours you, Lady Jaye, Roadblock, Barbecue, Destro, and the rest of his crazy outfit arrive at the designated location. Sector 7 is a barren valley surrounded by low hills.

"I don't see anyone," says Destro.

Lady Jaye pulls out her field glasses and scans the terrain. "There they are!" She points to the left.

Turn to page 90.

You lead Lady Jaye, Roadblock, and Barbecue to a position about twenty feet above the road. You drop down into a deep crevasse. The others follow you. Safely protected, the four of you wait. The rumble of the COBRA column is getting closer. A few seconds later the first tank comes into view. It passes right below your position; then a second one appears.

"Get ready," whispers Barbecue.

The third tank passes by.

"Get ready for what?" asks Roadblock. "Those tanks have us outnumbered, outgunned, and outclassed."

The fourth tank passes by.

You turn to Roadblock and ask, "What are we going to do?"

The fifth tank passes by. It stops. The main gun turret rotates slowly. The tank fires and the cliff explodes around you. Roadblock yells, "Right now we're not going to do a whole lot!"

Lady Jaye and Roadblock dive behind an outcropping of rock. You and Barbecue follow. You open fire on the COBRA tanks, but it's no good. You're not only outnumbered, outgunned, and outclassed, you're out of time.

A COBRA missile screams through the air, aimed directly at your location.

G.I. Joe mission over—but not accomplished.

THE END

Driving the H.I.S.S. tank, you approach the High-Security Area. Automatically an armored door slides open to reveal an enormous room. In the cool blue light, you make out rows and rows of highly advanced electronic processing equipment.

"This must be it," you whisper to Thunder. "Anything as big as Dragon Fire would require this kind of support equipment. This is definitely it!"

"Well, what are we waiting for? Let's short-circuit this operation!"

You ease the H.I.S.S. tank into the room. The door slides shut behind you. "There's so much here," you say, "I don't know where to begin."

Suddenly a voice comes over your radio. "It is quite impressive, I know. Perhaps you should take a moment to enjoy it."

"Who is this?" you demand. "Identify yourself!"

"You come all this way to investigate my operation and you don't even know who I am? You really should have been briefed in greater detail."

Thunder's trigger finger begins to twitch. "That's COBRA Commander," he says. "The big banana himself! He's got a bad attitude. I say it's time we teach him a lesson!"

Go on to page 57.

Thunder centers his sights on the biggest computer complex in the world. When they're locked in, he punches the button. The main cannon roars, and you brace yourself for the explosion—but nothing happens.

"How could I have missed? It's right in front of us." Thunder fires another shell, but again there's no hit.

A wicked laugh comes over the radio. "There is a good reason why my computers remain undamaged." Suddenly the entire scene vanishes, and you're left staring into black space. "What you have just seen was a multidimensional laser projection of my operation. The actual Dragon Fire control center is still fully protected. And it will remain that way."

Turn to page 62.

You call out to Duke, "When everything is sorted out back there, come up front. I know where we're going."

Duke runs up to you with the rest of the column rolling behind him. He jumps into the front seat and you hit the ignition switch. The COBRA APC rumbles to life.

You point to the topographic screen and say, "This area is dark because the data base for it was erased. It's got to be top secret."

"You're probably right on that point," says Duke. "Let's roll!"

You slip the transmission into gear and lay on the gas. *CRASH!* The APC leaps back, ramming the jeep behind you.

Duke looks over at you. "Spider, my good friend, a COBRA armored personnel carrier is not a Volkswagen. Why don't I drive? You can sit over here and use this electrical gadgetry to navigate."

Is he kidding? If he thinks you can't even drive an APC, how does he expect you to help uncover Dragon Fire? On the other hand, Duke *is* the acting first sergeant.

. . . .

If you ignore Duke, ram the transmission into the proper gear, and peel on out, turn to page 78.

If you switch seats with Duke, turn to page 19.

58

You call out from the communications bunker, "Yo, Destro! Come in here! I want to talk."

"What are you up to?" Lady Jaye asks.

"I'm getting out of this mess! And if joining a rebel outfit is what it takes, then that's what I'm going to do."

Roadblock rattles his handcuffs. "You're lucky that I'm wearing these, you traitor!" he says.

"Now, what's this?" Destro says, standing in the doorway. "Bitterness and unrest in the Joe Team?" He chuckles. "So you want to join our honorable...organization, Spider?"

"That's right," you answer. "These losers turn my stomach." You flash an icy look at Roadblock, Barbecue, and Lady Jaye.

Destro eyes you. "You changed your mind pretty fast, G.I. Joe. What's wrong? You don't like the accommodations?"

"I just had a little change of heart."

"Very well," says Destro. "But no funny stuff. My men will be watching you—through their gun sights, understand?"

You nod.

Destro motions to one of his guards. "Unlock this man."

As they release your arms you look up at Destro and say, "There is one thing...my weapon and ammo."

"Of course," says Destro. "You'll need it."

Turn to page 87

59

KA-BLAM! A second blast rips into the road in front of you. Roadblock cuts sharply to the left.

"Where are they coming from?" shouts Barbecue.

Dirt and rocks shower down around you. "They're being launched from behind us," you answer.

BOOM! Another rocket hits just off to the side. The blast nearly throws you out of your seat. "We're being chased by the COBRA tanks!" yells Lady Jaye.

"They're doing more than just chasing us," Roadblock answers. "They're using us for target practice." The road in front of you lifts up into the air as another round strikes home. "And I do believe they're getting better!" he shouts. You can barely hear him, there's so much noise.

Barbecue moves closer and screams, "We're no match for their fire power! A few more tries and they'll have us zeroed in."

You think fast. You can either stay on the road and outrun them, or cut down into the ravine and try to lose them. You've got to tell Roadblock which way to go.

....

If you decide to tell Roadblock to outrun the column, turn to page 12.

If you decide to tell Roadblock to lose 'em in the ravine, turn to page 26.

60

The voice on the radio has taken you by surprise, but you manage to ask it, "What's going to stop us from going after the real Dragon Fire?"

"Well, for one thing, even the floor that you drove out on was a laser projection. If you could check the outside, you'd see that your tank is currently resting on a narrow steel beam. Any movement you make will upset the balance. However, since I don't want you to sit there with nothing to do, I shall provide some entertainment."

From his unseen position, COBRA Commander reactivates the lasers. Several scenes from both inside and outside the Command Center appear. Then, slowly, COBRA Commander himself materializes in front of the tank. "First you can watch as I deal with the G.I. Joe Team and that troublesome Destro. Then"—his voice lowers—"you may watch as I begin to fool the whole world."

THE END

You let go of the roll bar, reach down, and hit the brake switch. *SCREECH!* Both tracks lock up, causing the back end of the APC to fly around. There's nothing anyone can do now. You tumble down the hill, flipping end over end over...

END.

Roadblock is under the truck, Duke, Barbecue, and Rock 'n' Roll are by the water's edge, and you and Lady Jaye are up on the bank. Everything is ready.

A few minutes later a patrol boat comes down the river. All goes according to plan. The boat passes by, circles around, then pulls up along the bank. One COBRA stays at the wheel as three others climb ashore. As soon as they're out in the open, you let loose a round of fire while Duke and the others rush the boat and get rid of the COBRAS. In a few seconds it's over. You've captured the patrol boat.

With Duke at the helm, you pull out into the current and race down the river. You check out the craft. There are twin .50-caliber machine guns up front, rockets mounted on the sides, and a double rack of depth charges off the stern. Below deck are a pair of H & R diesels. Top speed is 32 knots. It's a nice little boat.

You move to the cockpit and turn on the radar. The screen lights up. "There's a lot of traffic about a mile downstream," you say. "It could be the base port."

Turn to page 68.

You land silently on the cold stone floor. Then, rolling quickly away, you begin to close in on COBRA Commander.

About thirty yards from your prey you back around a double-phase switching box and then, swinging up to an overhead power cable, you pull yourself onto an elevated access ramp. A group of technicians is coming straight toward you. Slipping quietly over the side, you hang from the edge until they pass. When it's safe, you pull yourself back onto the walkway and move quickly to a point above the observation monitor. COBRA Commander is directly below you.

Turn to page 25.

The combined forces of the G.I. Joe Team and Destro's rebels will knock out the heavy artillery that protects COBRA Command Center. Your objective is four hours away over rugged mountainous terrain. On the way, you check over your equipment while keeping a sharp eye on Destro's men.

You cross a mountain ridge and catch sight of your objective. Readings from the trajectory analyzer show that the COBRA position is still out of missile range. Hawk gives the order to move closer. With Destro's men on the left flank and the G.I. Joes on the right, you advance on the big guns.

But suddenly the COBRAS open fire. As the shells pound in around you, the Joe Team sets up and begins firing back.

"What's going on?" yells Hawk. "Our rounds are way off their mark. Spider, Thunder, check your sights!"

"It's no good!" you answer. "The electrical circuits that control the trajectory are being jammed. We can't override them."

Off to the side, unnoticed because of this development, two of Destro's men sneak over the top of the hill. One of them carries a small black box. It's probably got some kind of fancy technical name. Whatever it's called, it did a good job of jamming your circuits. In fact, thanks to Destro and his little box, this whole mission is short-circuited right here!

THE END

66

You work your way back to Roadblock, Barbecue, and Lady Jaye. On a ridge overlooking the camp, you pause just long enough to check things out. Everything looks quiet, so you move closer. At the outer perimeter there's still no sign of COBRA or Destro. You edge up to the abandoned communications bunker. Silently you creep to the entrance; then, barely breathing, you peer around the door and look inside. Roadblock, Barbecue, and Lady Jaye are just as you left them. You have to smile.

"Some act we put on," says Barbecue. "Destro bought it completely."

Roadblock nods his head. "I think I'll look into a movie career when we get through here."

"I'm sure you'll be a star," you say. "But first I'll have to get you guys loose." You scrounge around for a piece of metal and pry off the locks. As the prisoners rub the feeling back into their hands, you begin work on the radio transmitter. "With a few adjustments we should be able to make contact with Hawk and the rest of the G.I. Joe Team," you say.

Turn to page 75.

"That's probably where they've been taking all the Dragon Fire equipment," says Duke. "If we take care of that base port, it's a good bet that COBRA will be out of business."

He cuts the engine as the port comes into view. "We'll cruise by once just to get the layout," Duke says.

As Duke maneuvers closer, you all scan the port. There are six concrete docks. Tied alongside are thirty or forty barges waiting to be unloaded. You borrow Lady Jaye's binoculars and get a closer look at the cargo. Everything is marked "Thermal Control Station." On shore is a large generating facility. Off to the side you can see a fuel dump.

Turning the patrol boat around, Duke says, "That's our target, all right. Let's put them out of business!"

Turn to page 31.

Bazooka is your partner on the two-man team. Together you carry four hundred feet of climbing rope to a spot on the cliff that's directly over the COBRA compound. After checking your equipment, you secure the rope, clip it into your harness, and back over the edge of the cliff.

You touch ground lightly. A few seconds later Bazooka drops down beside you. "That part was easy," he says. "Now for the wall."

There are no guards in sight. Slinging your weapon over your shoulder, you and Bazooka scale the wall. You throw your leg over the top, and drop down inside the compound.

You're very close to one of the back service bays where several large COBRA trucks are being unloaded. "Dressed like this, we're sure going to stand out," says Bazooka. "But if we borrow some of those white coats from the workers, we might be able to walk right inside."

"It's worth a try," you say.

Creeping along the side of the building, you come up behind two of the COBRA workers. As they turn around to lift a large crate, you jump them. Then you borrow their uniforms and take their places on the job.

"This stuff is top secret!" whispers Bazooka.

"Yeah," you answer, "and we're helping them move it."

....
Turn to page 43.

Pushing the hydraulic controls into forward, you say, "Next stop, COBRA Commander's private office!" You lurch forward and begin to climb up the tank in front of you.

"How did you learn to drive one of these?" asks Thunder.

"I didn't." You give it the gas and make it up over the first tank. Then the massive tank rams through COBRA's main wall.

"Well, you're doing all right for the first time out," Thunder says. Then he adds, "Hold it a second. I want to open the gate." He rotates the tank's turret until its main cannon is aimed directly at the gate in COBRA's wall. "This will do it," he says. He punches the button labeled "Fire." *KA-BLAMM!*

Thunder checks his sights and says, "Piece of cake. Here come the other tanks, and the Joe Team is right behind them."

"Well, let's get going before they run us down," you say. You spin the tank around and charge across the compound, heading straight for the Command Center. Fifty yards away you call, "Thunder, let 'em have it!" He loads another shell from the automatic magazine and fires it off. *WHAM!*

From your driver's sights you can see that the door to COBRA Command Center is just twisted metal, hanging off its hinges.

Turn to page 14.

As the smoke slowly clears, a fiendish laugh fills the room. It's COBRA Commander! He's hit, but he has time to gloat over his wicked scheme.

"You're too late. Dragon Fire has just been released. My plan to terrorize the world is now a reality. Major cities will soon be destroyed by tremendous geysers of steam caused by geothermal pressure inside the earth. And there's nothing you can do to stop it!" COBRA Commander sinks to the floor.

"It's not over yet, you say."

Your teammates drag COBRA Commander away from his computer bank and you take his place. Checking the program, you announce, "He's telling the truth. Pressure is building under major cities around the world. Somebody give me the readouts from the geodynamic analyzer." Duke calls out a string of numbers, and you enter them into the program. "Now give me the coordinates of the Morasis fault line in the Pacific Basin."

"27-36 by 1400-12," he calls out.

"This is going to be close," you say, "but we'll just have to take a chance!"

You enter the code, then lean back and watch the second hand move around the clock.

Forty-two seconds later you announce proudly, "We've done it! According to the stratospheric sensors, all of the Dragon Fire power has been harmlessly diverted through an extinct volcano on the coast of New Guinea. This COBRA crisis is over!"

THE END

Lady Jaye slips off to the left and disappears into the rough terrain.

Half a dozen tanks roll by. There's a minute of quiet. Then another tank roars up.

"Get ready," you whisper. "This could be it."

Roadblock checks his equipment, patting his armored vest to be sure everything is in place. You take a deep breath. Barbecue flashes you the thumbs-up sign.

Suddenly a sharp voice barks out, "COBRA driver, pull this vehicle over to the side. This is an authorized safety inspection."

"That's our cue," says Roadblock. "Let's do it!"

Turn to page 82.

You move two steps closer to Destro and say, "We aren't exactly eager to join up with a rebel outfit led by an overdressed dynamite dealer, but it seems to be the best move we can make. We're with you."

"Fine," says Destro. "Let's decide on a strategy." He walks over to the map taped to the wall. "This is the location of COBRA Command Center. Somewhere within the complex is the central geothermal control room. My latest intelligence indicates that Dragon Fire is not yet fully operational. But there isn't a lot of time. I suggest that we move out immediately."

"I don't know," says Barbecue. "I'd feel better if we could try to contact the others. We could certainly use the extra fire power. What do you think, Spider?"

If you want to move out fast, turn to page 54.

If you think it's better to try to contact the others first, turn to page 46.

While you fiddle with the dials, a deep voice comes through the speaker. "Since someone is fooling with this transmitter, I must presume that the three of you have freed yourselves. Probably with the help of Spider."

"That's Destro," says Lady Jaye. "He's been monitoring us."

The voice continues, "Unfortunately, by incorrectly taking the transmitter out of emergency mode, you have armed the camp's self-destruct mechanism. You have about five seconds. Goodbye."

Roadblock looks at you and Barbecue. Lady Jaye yells, "Run!"

But she's too late. You've run out of time and you've run out of luck. So long, Operation Dragon Fire. So long, Spider!

THE END

Immediately you respond in code:

REPEAT MESSAGE. REPEAT MESSAGE.

Nothing. Turning to Thunder, you say, "Something has gone wrong. The tanks are in trouble!"

"We've got orders to stay put and mind the electronics," says Thunder, shaking his head. "But those men need some help. What do you think?"

· ·

If you decide to remain at your post, turn to page 53.

If you decide to help Destro's men, turn to page 85.

Destro is standing about five paces away. His arms are folded over his chest. Your plan of attack is ready. You approach him slowly and begin to deliver your answer, speaking slowly, lulling him with your voice. As he listens you watch him closely. When his eyes begin to look glazed—*POW!* You snap out a stinging back fist to his temple! Stunned, he falls to the ground.

Roadblock, Barbecue, and Lady Jaye are surprised by your fast attack, but when you call out "Let's get out of here!" they're right behind you. The four of you charge out of the bunker, but the guards are waiting for you. Caught in the crossfire, you don't stand a chance.

"Great job we did!" you shout to Roadblock as you dodge bullets. Roadblock mutters something about the "old college try."

You don't even try to smile. Your mission is over. And COBRA Commander may soon rule the world.

THE END

"I can drive," you growl at Duke.

"Okay, okay," he says. "No sweat, Spider."

All goes well until—*BAM! BAM! BAM!* A COBRA sniper lets loose a rain of fire on you and the others.

The next thing you know, your APC is pitching over a cliff. You black out. When you come to, Duke is nowhere in sight, the APC is a mass of flames, and the last of the G.I. Joe Team are tearing ahead, out of range of the sniper.

You spend a few minutes looking in vain for Duke, then drag yourself to your feet and start walking. You're careful to stay as hidden as possible, out of sight from snipers.

After what seems like hours, you think you hear voices. You flop down and belly-crawl over a rocky rise of land. You can't believe what you see! It's a COBRA camp, but the entire main G.I. Joe patrol is there—even Duke. And he's talking to Destro!

You're suspicious. Destro is not to be trusted. He's a COBRA weapons supplier, but he's no more loyal to COBRA than he is to anyone else.

Go on to page 79.

You creep closer and duck behind a boulder. Thunder is standing not far away. "Psst!" you hiss. "Thunder! What's going on?"

Thunder runs over to you and starts to call out your name, but you silence him. "What is this? What are you and Duke and the others doing with Destro?"

Thunder explains that after the Joe Team drove off, they were stopped by Destro and a band of heavily armed COBRAs who are working for him. Destro has uncovered Operation Dragon Fire. It's a plot of COBRA Commander's to destroy the large cities of the world using the powerful geothermal force of the earth's internal heat. Destro wants the project stopped; if it continues, COBRA will no longer need his weapons.

Destro has found out where the COBRA Command Center is, and he's trying to convince Duke and the others to join forces with his rebels and put a stop to Dragon Fire.

You are skeptical, but you step out from behind the boulder.

"Spider!" Duke is glad to see you. "I gave you up for dead," he says.

He introduces you to Destro. Apparently Duke has already decided to trust him. They're making plans to attack the main compound of the COBRA Command Center, using stolen COBRA H.I.S.S. tanks. There's nothing for you to do but go along.

Turn to page 49.

You look around the circle and say, "We'll slip on board one of the barges." Duke gives your decision the okay.

You don't have to wait long. Moving slowly down the river is a COBRA barge. You and the others slip into the river. With just your eyes and nose above the water, you watch the barge come closer. You don't see any crates of machinery on this one. That seems odd, but it's so close now that you can't move or say anything—it might give away your position.

As the barge drifts by, you reach out and take hold of the side. The others do the same. Everything seems quiet on deck.

You're about to pull yourself on board when something grabs you from below. It's got your legs! You try to twist free, but you're pulled under the water. Using your knife, you manage to fight your way back to the surface. This time you see your attacker. It's a COBRA diver—one of the underwater Eels. Sputtering for breath, you try to call out a warning to the others, but the Eel attacks again, and before a sound can come out of your throat, you're pulled below the surface. Unless your other G.I. Joe teammates can escape, no one may ever know what Operation Dragon Fire is . . . until it's too late.

THE END

You, Roadblock, and Barbecue charge up the ravine. Lady Jaye has stopped a COBRA personnel carrier with four troopers in it. She's got her boot propped up on the front tire and one hand on her hip. The other hand is pointing into the driver's face. "You're in a lot of trouble," she barks. "Let's see some identification."

The driver can't believe this is happening, and that's all the diversion the rest of you need. Coming up from behind, you jump the troopers on the left. Roadblock and Barbecue take the ones on the right. You toss them out onto the road.

Before they can recover, Roadblock jumps into the driver's seat. You and Lady Jaye and Barbecue are right behind him.

You glance over your shoulder as the APC peels out. The four COBRA troopers are sitting in the dust. "I don't think they even know what hit them," you tell Roadblock.

"That's not surprising," says Lady Jaye. "When you jump the last vehicle in a column, you usually get away clean and neat."

"And that's just what we did," says Barbecue. "And now that we've got some wheels, we can check out this COBRA business in style."

Turn to page 8.

You start explaining to Bazooka. "We happen to be hiding under a signal master 6000-RX. It's an industrial-quality broadcast system used for internal communication. I could bridge over from these output sections, run it into this line, and then drive it out with a double-strapped amplifier. If it was all channeled into that computer room, the volume of sound would turn their circuits into electronic spaghetti. Unfortunately, I need a signal source, something to make some noise."

"How about this?" asks Bazooka. He pulls a cassette out of his inner pocket. "Let's give it a try."

Eagerly you start clipping cables and jumping connections. You're so busy that you don't notice the COBRA guards coming back into the room.

"G.I. Joes, halt!" a voice barks.

You and Bazooka whip around. Two COBRA troopers are towering over you, weapons drawn.

"I think COBRA Commander would be very interested in meeting you," says the other trooper.

You can feel Bazooka glaring at you.

"Well, it seemed like a good idea at the time," you tell him. The troopers prod you out of the computer room, their guns at your backs. You leave Dragon Fire behind, wondering if Duke and the others will be able to complete the mission. But for you the mission is over.

THE END

"And what's that other material?" asks Lady Jaye. "One of the radioactive isotopes?"

"Unfortunately, no," says Destro. "It is water. Simple, ordinary water. The steam that is generated will build to such extreme pressure that—"

"Like a wet rock next to a campfire, COBRA Commander could blow apart the earth from the inside out," Roadblock says.

No one says anything. Why are the others taking this horrible news so calmly? Is the story too farfetched to believe? Or are they just used to this kind of deathly dangerous situation?

"So are you with me?" Destro asks. "Do you believe I'm telling you the truth?"

....

If you believe Destro's story, turn to page 4.

If you want to find out more information and get a better handle on things before you answer, turn to page 37.

"Come on, Thunder!" you yell. "Let's give them a hand."

"They might need more than just a hand!" Thunder reaches under his seat and pulls out a small satchel of high explosives. Slinging it over his shoulder, he joins you alongside the truck.

The tanks are a few hundred yards away—just in front of the narrow entrance to the main gate of COBRA Command Center. But they're not moving.

"They're all jammed up behind the number-two tank!" says Thunder.

"I don't think there's anyone inside it," you say. "It looks abandoned. There isn't a lot of cover between us and the tanks...."

Thunder is staring at all the open ground the two of you must cover. Then he nods and yells, "Let's do it!"

You and Thunder take off, racing toward the tanks. The COBRA gunners behind the wall concentrate their fire on you.

Turn to page 45.

That blast tore through like an avalanche, and rocks and debris rolling down from above jammed up the low ground. If there's a way back to the main column, it's probably along the high ground.

You begin scaling the cliffs. It's not easy. Visibility is low. And the way back to the entrance is anybody's guess. You can't even be sure it's still there. The explosion might have sealed it over.

You feel your way onto a narrow ledge. It's just wide enough for you to stand on. One step at a time, your face flat against the cliff, you follow it to the left, feeling your way through the thick dust.

Five feet away, waiting quietly, waiting patiently, is a COBRA sniper. He bides his time, knowing you can't see him. For once he can afford to wait until his prey is within ideal range. When you are just two feet away from him, he opens fire. You don't have a chance to draw your weapon. As you pitch forward and crash down the rocky cliff, you realize that you never even got close to the COBRA plot. You hope the others will have better luck. The last thing you're aware of is the COBRA sniper shouting after you, "So long, sucker!"

THE END

A few moments later one of the guards returns with your M–16. You fire a few rounds into the air to make sure it's in working order.

"Good enough," you say. "Let's get going."

Destro and his men break down the rocket launchers and load the rest of their gear into jeeps and armored trucks. Five minutes later you move out.

You're riding in the second truck with a fellow called Rat-Lip or something. As the convoy moves up a rugged mountain pass, you check your watch. You're ten minutes out of camp. That's just about right. You reach behind the seat and grab the hand-held rocket launcher, then jump out of the truck. As you race up the rugged hillside, you call back, "Thanks for the lift, but I left something back at the camp."

Immediately Destro's men open fire. You dive for cover. As the bullets kick into the dirt, you set up the launcher. When it's adjusted and loaded, you take aim and fire. The rocket explodes fifty yards behind the last truck, blowing a huge crater into the road.

"Try to get around *that*!" you call out to Destro, in case he has any thoughts about coming back for you. You snake your way up the hill and disappear in the rocks.

Turn to page 67.

With flames shooting up into the air and the COBRA attack sirens wailing, you head for your last target: the thermal control station.

Lady Jaye gives you the target coordinates. You cruise along until you're well within range. The shore battery opens up. *BLAM! BLAM!* You take a direct hit that shakes the boat, but Duke manages to hold the course.

Finally he raises his hands and yells, "Fire!"

You punch the button and six missiles streak to the target. The whole thermal control station trembles and shakes—then erupts in a massive geyser of steam.

"Bye-bye, Dragon Fire!" shouts Barbecue.

Duke swings the patrol boat out of the harbor. Behind you are the smoking remains of COBRA's Dragon Fire. Ahead of you is the way home.

THE END

Destro strides out to meet his contact.

Lady Jaye continues to peer through her binoculars. "I don't like this," she says. "The one standing on the right is the Baroness. She's COBRA's top intelligence officer. I just don't think she would betray COBRA Commander to work with someone like Destro."

"You're making me uneasy," says Barbecue.

Destro moves closer to the Baroness. Suddenly she raises her hand, and Destro stops in his tracks. A battalion of COBRAs has just moved over the hilltops.

Roadblock groans. "The whole bunch of us have been set up...and had. I think I want to do this over."

But it's too late. COBRA Commander has won—for now. Unless your G.I. Joe teammates can uncover Dragon Fire themselves, COBRA will soon rule the world.

THE END